AN UNOFFICIAL

DIARY OF A
ROBLOX

PRO

MEGA SHARK

By Ari Avatar

SCHOLASTIC INC.

© 2023 Scholastic Australia

First published by Scholastic Australia Pty Limited in 2023.

All rights reserved. Published by Scholastic Inc., *Publishers since 1920*. SCHOLASTIC and associated logos are trademarks and/or registered trademarks of Scholastic Inc.

The publisher does not have any control over and does not assume any responsibility for author or third-party websites or their content.

ISBN 978-1-339-00862-2

10 9 8 7 6 5 4 3 2 1   24 25 26 27 28

Printed in the U.S.A.   37

This edition first printing, January 2024

Cover design by Hannah Janzen and Ashley Vargas

Internal design by Paul Hallam

Typeset in Dawet Ayu, Silkscreen, LOGX-10, Apercu Mono, and Ate Bit

FRIDAY NIGHT

"Bruh, pass the Hawaiian **PIZZA**," Zeke said, reaching out his hand.

I picked up the warm pizza box and handed it to Jez, who then passed it on to Zeke.

"Pepperoni down here!" I replied.

Zeke took a slice of Hawaiian pizza then picked up the pepperoni box. He handed it to Jez, who took a piece for herself before passing it on to me. I selected a slice with a really puffy crust and took a **BIG** bite.

NOM, NOM, NOM!

We were at my place, sitting on the living room floor and using Mom's coffee table to eat off. My best avatar friends, Zeke and

Jez, had come over for Friday night pizza and a **MOVIE.**

"So, what are we watching tonight?" Jez asked between mouthfuls.

I pulled up our options on the television and highlighted one of them. "I was thinking this one," I said, giving them a mischievous smile.

"EPIC!" Jez and Zeke said at the same time.

We'd made a habit of having regular Friday night pizza and **MOVIE NIGHTS,** and we always liked to choose something a bit scary. Two weeks ago, we'd watched a zombie movie at Zeke's place. But tonight we were watching *The Hunt*.

I jumped up and dimmed the lights, then I selected the movie and the opening scene began with a shot deep within a dark ocean. The music was quiet and low. I could tell already that this was going to be a **CREEPY MOVIE.**

The camera came up out of the water to pan across the surface of the sea, and a silver fin cut through the water with deadly speed. The scene changed. We watched as if we were under the sea looking up at the surface. Suddenly, a figure swam across the screen. It was clearly a person, out for a leisurely swim in the ocean.

The music **PULSED** a low, ominous beat.

I heard Zeke draw in a sharp breath. "Bruh, that swimmer is **TOAST.**"

Jez and I nodded in agreement.

The swimmer kept gliding across the water, oblivious to the shark that began to move toward him. The music got faster and faster.

"OH NO!" Jez yelled.

The camera angle suddenly switched back to the surface of the water. The man's face turned to **HORROR** as he recognized what was in front of him. Then the screen filled up with giant, flashing teeth.

"AAAAAAGH!" we screamed in unison with the man on the screen.

"What's going on in here?" a voice called through the doorway.

"Dad, you're ruining the tension!"

I complained, pausing the movie.

"Seriously? *The Hunt?!*" he said, appalled. "That movie is the worst!"

"You only say that because of your job," I said. "You get all obsessed with the scientific facts and always point out what isn't right. It's meant to be fiction," I said, annoyed.

Dad is a marine biologist and studies creatures in the sea. He often goes out on boats to study dolphins, fish, sharks, and sea vegetation. But his real passion is keeping endangered sea animals safe.

"Ari, it's not just that it's not scientifically accurate," Dad said. "It's portraying a really negative image of **SHARKS.**"

"No offense, Mr. Avatar, but I don't need a movie to tell me sharks are negative," Zeke said, shivering. "I already know they would **EAT ME** alive!"

"Zeke, the ocean is their home. When you go in the sea, you are entering their domain. They need respect, not silly movies that portray them as mindless **KILLERS.** They're just trying to survive," Dad said.

I rolled my eyes across my block face and turned back to the screen. I pressed Play and the movie came to life again. The shark continued flailing about, tossing its victim around in its jaws. The man managed to break free and tried to swim away by diving downward. The shark flipped upside down and swam after him.

"That's so **FAKE,**" Dad said, folding his arms. "Sharks don't intentionally swim upside down. Whenever they're flipped, they enter a kind of **TRANCE.** It's called tonic immobility and it makes them completely calm and still."

"**DAD!**" I yelled, pausing the screen again. "You're ruining the movie!"

Jez smothered a giggle.

"OK, OK, I know when I'm not wanted," he said, holding up his hands. "But if you avatars are still coming out with me on the boat on Sunday, I need you to be a little more scientific in your approach to marine life than what this **GARBAGE** is teaching you."

Dad turned and walked out of the room. Jez **LAUGHED.**

"It's not funny," I said, irritated.

"It is a bit funny, Ari," she said. "And anyhow, he's right. I'm super pumped to go on his work boat to help tag some marine life this Sunday."

"Yeah, and maybe this wasn't the best movie to watch right before we go on an ocean trip," Zeke added, looking at the **SHARP TEETH** paused on the TV screen.

Hmm. Maybe he was right.

"OK, fair enough," I said, flicking back to the contents page. "How about *Zombie Dogs II*?"

"Yeah, **AWESOME,**" Jez said.

Zeke nodded.

I pressed a button and the new movie began to play.

Zeke was right. Maybe we shouldn't have watched that movie, because now I couldn't get the image of the **SHARK'S JAWS** with shining, razor-sharp teeth out of my head.

SATURDAY MORNING

I threw the ball across the
yard and Coda ran after it
with a happy **BARK.** She ran back
and dropped it at my feet.

"Good girl!" I said, ruffling her fur.

She sat and waited patiently,
hoping I would throw the ball
again.

So I did. I threw it across the

yard and she scampered after it happily.

"Hey, Ari!" I heard my dad's voice call from inside the house. "Come here for a minute."

"I'll be back, girl," I said to Coda, who let out a disappointed whimper.

I went inside and walked through to Dad's study. He was on his **LAPTOP** and was preparing for the trip out to sea with me and my friends the next day.

"Take a look," he said, pointing

to the screen. "We're going to be tagging some **DOLPHINS** tomorrow," he said, smiling.

"Dolphins! Cool!" I said excitedly. Sometimes when I went with my dad on his sea trips, we ended up doing boring things like looking at a new species of seaweed. But this time we were going to **SWIM** with dolphins. IRL!

"Why do you tag them?" I asked. "Isn't that painful?"

"No, no, it doesn't hurt them at all. But it does allow us to **TRACK** them on our computers. Which means we can learn more about where they go in different seasons, about their behavior in their groups, and more about their diets. This is super important if we want to protect them as a species."

I nodded.

"But this is the fun bit," he said with a smile. "There's a theory that dolphins are attracted to particular sounds, so we've been experimenting with how they respond to different musical instruments. If we can find a specific pitch that attracts them, we can use it to herd them into safer zones if they are in danger."

Dad hit a button on his computer and a high-pitched flute rang out.

"That's a **PICCOLO,**" he said. "It's a type of little flute that has a nice high range. We think dolphins respond well to these types of sounds."

"Is that why they make those **SQUEAKING** sounds?" I asked.

Dad nodded. "The high-pitched whistle of the bottle-nosed dolphin travels far through the water to communicate with other dolphins."

I thought about the playful dolphins I'd seen in movies, swimming and leaping gracefully through the air. I really hoped we'd see one. But then my mind shifted back to the eerie, dark water from our movie last night. I swallowed hard as I remembered what we had seen. A **FLASH** of teeth ripped through my mind's eye.

"Dad," I said carefully, "will there be **SHARKS?**"

Dad **LAUGHED.** "Are there cars on a highway?"

I frowned.

"Of course there are sharks in the ocean. I told you last night. It's their home. But we are not going into any particularly dense shark regions, as far as I know. But if we did see one, we'd be well protected in the submersible."

The **SUBMERSIBLE** was the coolest underwater vehicle and my face brightened at the thought of getting to ride in it. It was like a little underwater car that we could drive around under the sea. It even had little claw arms that Dad could control from the inside, which could pick things up off the ocean floor and collect them for research.

"OK, well, as long as there are no Great White Sharks chasing us, then I think I'll be fine," I said, letting out a sigh.

"We're not likely to see Great Whites in the area we are going tomorrow. It's too warm for them now. Don't worry, Ari. I'll look after you," Dad said with a wink.

Mom **KNOCKED** on the office door. My little sister, Ally, was at her side.

"What time are you two heading off tomorrow?" Mom asked.

"Oh, **EARLY** this time. We want a whole day out on the boat, so we'll head out as soon as Zeke and Jez are dropped off at about seven in the morning," Dad replied. "Are you excited, Ari?"

I nodded enthusiastically.

"Better hope you don't get eaten by a shark like the swimmers in that movie you were **TOO SCARED** to finish," Ally taunted.

"We weren't too scared! We just thought it was boring," I said, my cheeks flushing red.

"Yeah right." Ally **LAUGHED.**

"You're just jealous that me and my friends will get to swim with dolphins!" I said.

"Dolphins?!" Ally squealed. "Dad, that's not **FAIR!** Dolphins are, like, my **FAVORITE** animal."

I smirked. Got her.

"Come on, Ally," Mom said, guiding my little sister away. "It's Ari's turn this time. How about we call your friends and do a picnic in the yard tomorrow? We can make cupcakes."

After they left, and despite Ally's taunts, I focused on the upcoming trip, and any remaining thoughts about sharks quickly left my mind. I felt a rush of excitement fill my body. Dolphins? Submersibles? It was going to be **EPIC!**

SUNDAY MORNING— VERY EARLY

"How are we doing, team? Almost ready?" Dad sang cheerily. There was always an extra spring in his step on the days he was going on an **EXPEDITION.** Even at seven o'clock on a Sunday morning.

"YEAH!" Jez, Zeke, and I chorused.

We piled into the car and Dad started up the engine. It wasn't too far a drive to the marina where Dad's expedition team would be waiting to help us get all our gear for the trip.

We drove along the highway, listening to Dad's specially created playlist, which involved every song known to avatars with the words "water," "sea," or "ocean" in its title.

After a short while, we exited the highway and took a long, winding road that descended down to the coastline.

"I can see the ocean!" Jez declared.

I craned my neck to see out of the front windshield, and sure enough, the deep blue ocean stretched out along the horizon, glistening like a **DIAMOND.**

Dad parked the car by the wharf and we jumped out. The boat shed had a big sign above it with Dad's company logo, which read "Bioblock Marine Research Foundation," with an image of a dolphin diving over the top of the words.

We walked inside the boat shed where some of Dad's colleagues were waiting.

"Hey, avatars!" one of the scientists said. I'd met him before—his name was Jim and he'd been working with Dad for years.

Dad shook Jim's hand and gave him a friendly pat on the back.

"Got your best assistants with you today?" Jim asked, winking at me and my friends.

"Only the best!" Dad **SMILED.**

"How are you, Ari?" Jim said, putting his hand up for a high five.

"Great!" I replied. "These are my friends, Jez and Zeke."

Jim high-fived the others.
"I remember you avatars from the scuba course we did last school break."

Jez and Zeke nodded. Last break, we'd done an **EPIC** scuba diving course with some of Dad's colleagues. We learned how to breathe in the underwater masks and use the oxygen tanks. It meant we now had our very own licenses to go scuba diving with Dad any time we liked.

"Well, let's get you some suits then!" Jim said cheerfully.

We followed Jim into the storeroom where he pulled out the **SCUBA SKINS** for us to wear. We held them up against our bodies, checking them for length. Then he gave each of us a pair of flippers and a diving mask.

We held on to our gear as we entered the office adjoining the boat shed. Dad was already inside, standing with two other colleagues and looking at maps on a computer, pointing to the different areas lit up on the screen.

"We've had quite a lot of **DOLPHIN ACTIVITY** in this region," one of the avatars said, pointing to the screen. He then dragged his finger across to the left. "And in this smaller region here. Team A can explore this second area, while Team B can take the larger spot with the submersible."

Dad turned to us and winked. We were Team B with Dad. Jim and the others were Team A and would be on another boat. Dad gathered some paper maps and other bits and pieces and gestured for us to follow him outside to the wharf. My stomach **FLIPPED** with excitement, like I had little avatars inside doing an epic obby course.

We walked down the wharf, which was lined with boats of all different sizes. I squinted as the sunlight bounced off the glistening ocean. We stopped outside a Bioblock company boat, which was moored down at the end. Jim and his crew were going on the slightly bigger boat anchored just next to ours. But the most exciting part was seeing the **SUBMERSIBLE** attached to the back of our boat. It was a little, bright yellow pod with claws sticking out the front. I couldn't wait to get inside it.

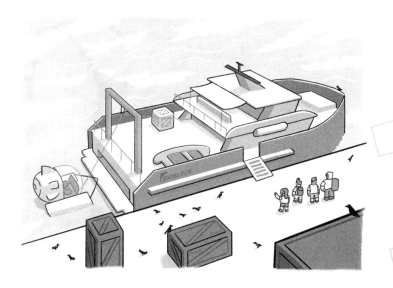

"ALL ABOARD!" Dad called.

"WOO-HOO!" Jez cheered, jumping onto the boat. Zeke and I followed.

There was a cabin at the front of the boat that contained a lot of tech equipment. I could see Jez—who is a total tech queen—practically drooling over the flashing screens. Just beyond the cabin was a big open deck leading out to the submersible that floated at the back of the boat.

"Who's ready to find some dolphins?" Dad yelled excitedly

as Jim's team launched their boat off behind us.

"YEAH!" we all sang.

I looked out to sea and wondered what fantastic creatures awaited us in the dark, mysterious blue.

SUNDAY—
MID-MORNING

Our boat sliced through the ocean quickly, **BUMPING** over waves and splashing us with sea spray. Zeke, Jez, and I laughed as we flipped and flopped all over the boat. After about an hour, Dad slowed the boat down and we began sailing a little more gently.

"Come here, avatars," he called from inside the cabin's **CONTROL ROOM.**

We went inside and saw Dad pointing to a flashing navigation system. Jez's eyes widened in excitement.

"So, we are here," he said, pointing to a map. "And here is where there has been a fair bit of dolphin activity lately."

"What's this dark section just there?" Jez asked, pointing to a shadow on the screen.

"That is super exciting," Dad said. "It's an **OLD MARINE**

RIG. It was decommissioned years ago and converted into a reef. It's now home to a lot of interesting marine life. And it's really fun to explore in your scuba gear." Dad winked.

"Epic!" we all yelled.

We filed out onto the deck to put on our wet suits and **SCUBA GEAR.**

Once our suits were on and Dad had set up our oxygen tanks, we were ready to go. He ran through the safety rules and the hand signals we could make to one another to communicate.

"I'm going to use these speakers to try and attract the dolphins," Dad said, pointing to his computer in the control room. "You avatars can go down to **EXPLORE** for a bit while I stay up here to test the different frequencies to attract the dolphins. You each have an **UNDERWATER CAMERA** on you, so I'll be able to see you the whole time."

"Are the dolphins tame?" Zeke asked, looking a little concerned.

"No, they're not tame, Zeke," Dad answered. "They are **WILD ANIMALS** and we need to respect them. But they are generally very friendly and playful, and I think you are going to enjoy meeting them. I've swum with a few pods around here and they love the researchers."

We put on our **BREATHING MASKS** and sat on the edge of the boat. Then on Dad's command, we all leaned backward and **PLOPPED** into the ocean.

The three of us **DOVE DOWN,**

gently kicking our flippers to propel us along. Zeke made a noise and pointed straight ahead. It was the sunken marine rig!

We swam over **EXCITEDLY** as the underwater playground came into view. It was a mass of rusted metal, covered in barnacles and coral. I beckoned the others to follow me as we swam through one of the old door openings.

It was **DARK** and eerie inside the rig. There were corridors and openings all around us. It was like swimming through a maze. I wouldn't want to get **LOST** down here!

We rounded a corner and entered what looked like an old control center. Colorful fish circled above the control panel, but they quickly scattered when Jez swam over to push some buttons. The panel remained dark.

Suddenly, I heard a high-pitched ringing. It sounded like the trill of a musical instrument. It must have been Dad testing sounds to see what would attract the dolphins. I gestured for the others to follow me out of the rig. It was beginning to **CREEP** me out.

We exited the sunken wreck and looked around. It was brighter outside the rig and we could see all kinds of marine life bustling around us. Jez wildly gestured and I followed her gaze to see a ginormous fish swimming by.

A dark shadow shifted on the sea floor and I startled. It was a **STINGRAY!** It rose from the bottom of the sea to gracefully glide past us, its long stinger following behind it like a tail.

We all looked at one another with wide eyes. This was **SO COOL.**

Suddenly, Zeke looked behind me with an expression of **ALARM.** His eyes were wide as he pointed, gesturing for me to turn around. There was something behind me. I could feel it approaching. So I turned, gasping in surprise.

"AAAAAAH!"

SUNDAY—
A BIT LATER

"DOLPHINS!" I exclaimed, my voice muffled by my breathing mask.

A pod of five beautiful dolphins came **SPEEDING** toward us. They swam around us in circles, then accelerated to the surface of the water toward the speaker on the boat.

So, they are attracted to that

sound. Dad would be stoked.

The dolphins came back down,
curious about their avatar visitors.

One of them swam right up to me
and pushed its body against me
like a cat against the legs of its

owner. I gently extended my hand and it swam its body along the palm of my hand. It was smooth and soft.

I turned to see Zeke reach out to touch another dolphin on its nose. He then swam away and the dolphin followed. The dolphin eventually caught up to Zeke and nudged him back with its nose. They were **PLAYING TAG!** Zeke swam around to try and tag the dolphin back but the dolphin was much too fast for him.

A smaller dolphin swam beneath

Jez and corkscrewed up toward the surface. We saw it break the surface of the water and do a **MASSIVE FLIP** before crashing back into the sea.

Dad would have loved seeing that from the boat.

When the dolphins had finished playing, they grouped together and then sped off into the distance.

I signaled to Jez and Zeke that it was time to go back to the surface. We swam up slowly, being careful not to ascend too fast as it could be dangerous. We broke through the surface of the water and pulled our mouthpieces out.

"That was so **EPIC!**" Jez yelled. "Did you see that dolphin flip? **OBBY DOLPHIN!**"

"Did you see me playing tag with that dolphin? He totally knew how to play!" Zeke laughed.

"I can't believe I actually touched a dolphin," I joined in joyfully.

"Well, that was quite an awesome experience, wasn't it?" Dad called from the boat. "I saw it all on your underwater cameras. I think you've made some new ocean friends."

We couldn't stop smiling as Dad helped us back onto the boat. We pulled off our wet suits and **FLOPPED** onto the deck, exhausted.

"I hope you're not too tired," Dad said. "Let's have a bite to eat and dry out your wet suits before we do the **NEXT THING** on our list."

"Which is?" Zeke asked.

Dad smiled brightly and nodded toward the back of the boat.

"The **SUBMERSIBLE!"**

SUNDAY—
AFTER LUNCH

After lunch, the sun dipped behind some gray clouds. Dad looked out to the horizon and frowned. Then he walked into the cabin's control room to look at the radars.

"Some unexpected weather on the way," he said. "We should probably get into the submersible soon. There's a **STORM** coming later and we want to make sure we're back to shore by then."

Dad walked out of the cabin to get the submersible ready. We were about to follow when Jez leaned toward one of the other radars.

"I wonder what that **BIG SHADOW** is?" she said, pointing.

I squinted at the screen, but I couldn't see anything—only Jez seemed to be able to read the radars. To me it was just a bunch of blinking shapes.

"THERE." She pointed again at the lights on the screen.

"Sunken wreckage stuff?" Zeke said, shrugging.

"But it's **MOVING,**" she said, leaning in.

"Dolphins?" I asked.

"No way," she said. "It's too big. Far too big to be any kind of marine animal, I would think."

"Submarine?" Zeke guessed.

"Maybe," Jez said, unconvinced.

"COME ON, AVATARS!" Dad called

from the back of the boat.

"I'm sure it's fine—Dad would have seen it," I said dismissively.

Jez frowned. "Maybe," she muttered again before shrugging and following us out of the cabin.

The **SUBMERSIBLE** bobbed around the surface of the water, with Dad, Jez, Zeke, and myself tucked neatly inside.
It was a lot bigger inside than I had expected, with seats for all of us. I'd never ridden in it before and had always wanted to.

The roof was a glass dome
so we could see all around us.
Dad shifted the gears and the
submersible **SANK** into the sea. I
instinctively held my breath as it
went under the waves, but
I didn't need to, of course.

I looked around the inside of the
submersible and saw a few boxes,
including one marked with a first
aid cross. There were controls
all across the dashboard that
flashed and beeped. Behind our
seats was a large chute with an
airtight door. It led to a tunnel
that could be used to exit the

submersible into the ocean without letting any water back inside. We'd all brought our scuba gear with us in case we wanted to **EXPLORE** outside the submersible.

Dad pushed the accelerator and we increased speed. We flew through the ocean like a car on a highway. Fish with puzzled expressions watched as this strange new sea creature **ZOOMED** by. We passed the abandoned marine rig and into a more open area and followed along the seabed until it dropped away. We had reached the continental shelf.

"Wow, what's down there?" Jez asked, eyeing the vast darkness.

"I don't really know," Dad said.
"It goes really deep and our
equipment can't track it all the
way to the bottom."

I swallowed **NERVOUSLY.**

Dad slowed the engine and the
submersible perched on the edge
of the drop-off. Dad maneuvered
the claws and started picking
things up from the seabed.

"Fascinating," he murmured, looking
at what the claw had picked up.
It looked like a boring old rock
to me.

Some time had passed before
Dad was seemingly satisfied
with the number of samples he
had collected. He retracted the
submersible's claws and looked
across at another radar.

"Oh, looks like the weather up
on the surface is getting a little
rough," Dad said. "We might have
to call it a day, avatars."

I breathed a sigh of relief. I didn't
like where we were.

Dad kicked the submersible into
gear and began to ascend, away

from the darkness beyond the
shelf. I was happy to be leaving
that dark hole behind.

But just as we were about to
come up over the top of the cliff
face, we were hit with a
gigantic . . .

BANG!

SUNDAY—
A BIT LATER

The submersible **TUMBLED** upside
down over and over, spinning
rapidly through the water. We
toppled around inside like clothes
in a washing machine.

"AAAAAGGGGGH!"

"What was that?!" Zeke screamed.

Dad tried to steady the
submersible. "I don't . . . I don't

know," he stammered.

He managed to turn the submersible upright. And that's when we all saw it. We were face to face with the **BIGGEST SHARK** I had ever seen— even bigger than the shark in our movie the other night. And it was racing toward us with its mouth wide open.

"AAAAAAAAGH!"

Dad kicked the submersible into gear and tried to drive it upward at top speed. But even I knew enough about sharks to know that we could never outswim one.

"Is that a **GREAT WHITE?**" I stammered.

"Possibly. But it's not like any I've ever seen before," Dad said breathlessly. "It's much closer to the extinct sharks of prehistoric times."

"That's a **DINO-SHARK?!**"
Zeke screamed.

"I don't know," Dad said. "But I
do know we won't get away by
driving straight. I'm going to need
to move us around a lot. She's big,
so I don't think she'll be able to
swim in sharp movements as well
as a normal-sized shark could.
Everyone, **STRAP IN.**"

We secured our seat belts and
Dad began moving the submersible
from left to right in **SHARP,**
confusing movements. I watched
the shark from the back of the

dome. She was following us with speed, but every time we took a sharp turn, she had to stop mid swim to turn. Dad was right—her body wasn't as nimble as the dolphins we'd played with earlier.

"Come on, Dad! Get us back to the boat," I pleaded, my voice shaking.

"I'm doing my best, avatars," he said. "I'll keep you safe."

"She's **GAINING** on us," Jez said nervously.

I looked behind again and the

shark seemed to anticipate our moves. She accelerated and came toward us at **LIGHTNING SPEED.** I looked straight into her cold, black eyes.

"DAD!" I yelled.

The shark's mouth was shut but she wasn't slowing down.

"She's going to **RAM US** again!" Zeke yelled.

"Brace yourselves!" Dad warned.

And then . . .

BANG!

The submersible **TUMBLED** through the ocean again like a ball in a pinball machine. The lights on the dashboard flashed and beeped, then suddenly went silent. The submersible slowly sank to the ocean floor, rolling along the sand until it came to a stop.

I touched a hand to my head where it was **PULSING** with pain. I must have bumped it somewhere along the way.

"Is everyone OK?" I croaked.

"Yeah," Jez and Zeke said in ragged breaths.

"What about you, Dad?" I called out. "Dad?"

I undid my seat belt and leaped over to my dad. His eyes were shut as he sat slumped in his seat.

Jez and Zeke bolted over to help.
Jez felt Dad's pulse and checked
his breathing. Zeke pointed to
a lump on his head.

"He's **UNCONSCIOUS,**
but he's breathing okay," Jez said.

"He needs to get to a hospital!"
I yelled desperately.

"Yes, he does," Jez agreed. "Let's
move him to the seats at the back.
We can lay him down and secure
him in the seat with the belts."

We awkwardly moved Dad across

the submersible and strapped him into the back seat.

"I'll keep an eye on him," I said with tears in my eyes.

"Ari, he'll be OK," Jez promised, squeezing my hand.

I really hoped she was right.

"Where—where's the dino-shark?" Zeke suddenly called out, panicked.

Somehow, in all the drama with Dad, we'd completely forgotten about the prehistoric **MEGA SHARK** lurking somewhere outside the submersible.

We looked around wildly at the vast ocean. No sign.

"Jez, can you **DRIVE** this thing?" I asked.

Jez looked at the controls and nodded. "I know this kind of system. I just need to **POWER** it up again."

She hit some keys but the dashboard remained dark.

"I think it has lost power," she said.

"Lost power?! But we need it to work so we can get back to the boat! I need to get Dad to a **DOCTOR!**" I cried.

"*And* there's a killer shark on the loose out there," Zeke added. "What are we going to do?!"

"OK, think," Jez said, tapping her head. "I can see the marine rig in the distance over there," she said, pointing through the dark ocean. "So at least we know where we are. The boat wasn't too far from there. We might have to swim back and radio for help."

"Ah, Jez," Zeke cried. "Do I need to remind you again about the **GIGANTIC SHARK** that wants to eat us?!"

"What other choice do we have?" Jez yelled back.

"GUYS! STOP YELLING!" I said, panting. "Jez is right. One of us needs to get to the boat. And it's my Dad who needs help. So—"

"Ari, no, you can't. It's way too

dangerous," Zeke interrupted.

"No," I said, shaking my head. "My Dad needs me."

I **CRAWLED** over to where we kept the scuba gear.

"I'm going out there."

SUNDAY—
EVEN LATER

"OK. I'm ready." I tried to make my voice sound steady.

Zeke checked over my scuba equipment a second time, just to make sure everything was right.

"I think your best bet is to swim for the marine rig," Jez said. "That will offer you the best **PROTECTION.** That shark is so big that she shouldn't be able

to fit in there. The swim to the
boat from the rig should be quick."

I nodded as I pulled my scuba
mask over my face.

I waddled over to the **EXIT
HATCH** in my flippers,
stumbling along the way.

"Are . . . are you sure about
this, Ari?" Zeke said quietly as
I readied myself to open the hatch.

I nodded firmly. My friends were
depending on me. My dad was
depending on me. Maybe even

for his life. I nodded over in his direction. "Just keep an eye on my dad, will you? Check his pulse and breathing and make sure he's OK."

"We will," Jez promised, pulling me into a hug.

I turned and hit the button to **OPEN** the hatch. It was like I had entered an elevator. The door closed quietly and I stood there in silence while I waited for the hatch to pull me out into the sea.

The tunnel opened and I was

SUCKED through the hatch and spat out into the ocean through a one-way flap. As water **RUSHED** in around me, the ocean seemed darker than it was before. The water also seemed to heave and pulse. I wondered if the storm had arrived.

My eyes darted from left to right, looking for any **OMINOUS SHADOWS.**

Just breathe.

I gently kicked my legs in the water, trying to swim with calm, rhythmic movements. I'd read somewhere that sharks could sense panic, and it attracted them to struggling prey. I didn't want to be struggling prey.

Suddenly, I saw something move in the corner of my eye. I **WHIPPED** my head to the side, but it was only a fish. It swam right past me and disappeared into the deep ocean beyond. I tried to keep my breathing even.

I focused back on my task and could see that the sunken marine rig was not too far ahead. If

I just calmly swam over there, I'd be in its **PROTECTION** within the next ten seconds.

A shiver ran down my spine.

I felt a presence.

A **LURKING** presence.

I searched behind me and saw nothing but the murky gray ocean. I looked side to side and couldn't see anything threatening, so I lowered my head and kept swimming.

I didn't get far before a long, ominous shadow covered me in darkness. I looked up and, to my horror, saw the shark swimming above me. It was **HUGE.**

I had to get to the rig.

I started to swim faster.

And faster.

I didn't want to, but I was
beginning to panic. My heart
THUNDERED in my chest and my
legs flailed about in desperate
kicks. The shadow above me
suddenly **DISAPPEARED,**
so I braved a look. The shark was
gone. I searched around me, but
she was nowhere. Nothing here
but an empty, murky ocean.

This isn't good.

I was so close to the rig I could almost touch it. But an almighty **WHOOSH** echoed in my ears as I suddenly tumbled through the water. The shark had launched herself at me from behind, but I had moved just in time. The force of her huge body moving past me so quickly had sent me spinning. She now floated between me and the safety of the rig, her **GIGANTIC TAIL** slapping against the opening to the rig's corridors.

I had to get around her.

As she maneuvered herself through the water to turn in my direction, I **LUNGED** for the opening of the rig just below her. The shark must have known what I was doing, because she angled herself downward to intercept my path. But her turn was too slow and I managed to slip through the narrow opening just as I felt the **IMPACT** of the shark hitting the rig's deck behind me.

She was too big to enter through this entrance. But I knew there were plenty of bigger openings throughout the rig that she could slip into. I needed to stick to the narrow corridors to get to the other side of the rig safely. Then it would only be a short, direct swim up to the boat.

As I swam through the corridors, I remained on high **ALERT.** But I came to a stop when the hall suddenly opened up into a large, vacant space—an entire section of the rig had eroded, leaving the space in front of me **EXPOSED** to the rest of the ocean.

I could see the corridor continue on the other side of the open space, which would lead me directly to the boat. I was almost there. I just had to get across.

I gulped.

Looking left and right, I swam out into the open. There were pieces of old equipment that lay decaying in the seabed cemetery of the rig. A massive **INDUSTRIAL FAN,** a control switchboard, and a series of pipes and tanks ran along the remaining walls.

I swam slowly—I just needed to stay undetected. But my stomach dropped as the looming dark shadow returned.

The enormous shark was **HURTLING** toward me like an underwater missile. Her jaws were **WIDE OPEN.**

SUNDAY AFTERNOON— LATER STILL

I **SCREAMED,** creating an explosion of bubbles from my mask. As the shark approached, I did a **BACKWARD SOMERSAULT,** kicking my flippers with all my might.

She narrowly missed me, and her momentum sent her **COLLIDING** with the huge fan. All she had to do now was turn around and I would be a goner. I'd never make it to the other side of the rig. This was it. I was **DOOMED.**

I closed my eyes and waited for the jaws of the shark to clamp down on me . . .

But nothing happened.

I opened one eye and saw the shark **STRUGGLING** in the water. Her tail fins were caught between the blades of the fan. She thrashed about, but I knew it wouldn't hold her for long.

I winced. But as the shark writhed, a thought **FLASHED** into my head. I remembered what Dad said on Friday night about the shark in our movie. It was something about sharks going into a **TRANCE** when upside down. What was it called? Tonic immobility?

I looked around. Just to the left of the fan was a switchboard with a giant lever. A small red light

flashed against the darkness.
It still had power!

BINGO!

Swimming over to the struggling
shark, I pulled the lever down
hard and the fan began to slowly
rotate. As it spun, the shark
FLIPPED over onto her back. I then
quickly stopped the fan by pushing
the lever back up, trapping her
upside down.

As if by magic, her thrashing
slowed and she calmed. She
floated, HYPNOTIZED.

This was my chance to escape.
I swam as fast as I could over to
the other side of the rig, through
the remaining corridor, and then
up to the surface of the water.
As I broke the surface, I was
SHOCKED to see big, swelling
waves pulsing up and down. Rain
pelted down from the blackened
skies. The storm had arrived. But

the worst part was what was in front of me. Or what wasn't in front of me, to be precise.

The boat was gone.

SUNDAY AFTERNOON— EVEN LATER

"NOOOOO!" I screamed into the sky. But my cries were muffled by the thundering of the storm.

Where was the boat?!

I realized that the huge waves must have pushed the boat away. We were **STRANDED.** There was no boat, no radio, and no help. And I was pretty sure the mega shark would break free from the fan soon, and I would be prey once again.

Dad's team members were sure to have figured out that we were missing, but how long would it take them to find us? And in the meantime, I was going to be **BOBBING** around the ocean like fresh bait on a hook.

I had to get back to the submersible.

DIVING back down, I reentered the rig and swam carefully through the center. I could see the broken fan on the far wall—but **NO SHARK.** She had gotten out!

I swam as fast as I could across the open part of the rig, then into the narrow corridors that would protect me from the shark. Once I reached the original entry point to the rig, I cautiously poked my head out. The bright yellow submersible was there in the distance. But no sign of the shark.

Taking a deep breath, I started to **SWIM.**

But just as I left the rig, the small groups of fish swimming peacefully around me began to scatter.

OH NO.

As I got closer to the submersible, I could see my friends **WAVING** their arms around in a panic. My heart skipped a beat as they confirmed my fears. Panicking, I swam like I'd never swum before, kicking my legs **FURIOUSLY.**

But it wasn't enough. I could feel her right at my feet. I wasn't going to make it.

Something heavy **CLAMPED DOWN** on my body. She'd got me! I readied myself for the pain of the bite—it was all over.

Then . . . nothing.

Wait, what?

I looked down and saw that it was the **CLAW** of the submersible, and not the jaws of a gigantic shark, that was clamped around my waist.

The claw **DRAGGED** me downward and fed me into the open hatch. After it released me, it retracted and the outer door closed. The hatch then drained of water and the inside door opened, giving me access to the submersible again.

I **COLLAPSED** on the floor, panting and crying. I ripped off my mask and pulled the wet suit off my arms with Zeke's help. I just wanted to get out of it.

"Bruh! You made it," Zeke said, pulling me into a hug.

"I was almost **SHARK BAIT**," I said, coughing out a little bit of water. "How's Dad?" I asked desperately.

"Ari," a voice croaked from the seats.

"DAD! YOU'RE AWAKE!" I yelled, racing over to him.

"I'm OK, son. Just a bump to the head. But I'll be OK."

I hugged him tightly.

"Bad news," I said. "The boat is gone. The storm must have taken it. We're **STUCK** here."

Dad closed his eyes and winced. "I can't believe I've put you avatars in so much danger," he said.

"It's OK, Dad," I said. "It's not your fault. You couldn't have predicted that a shark would cut the . . ." I trailed off. "Wait—I thought we didn't have power? How did you get **THE CLAWS** working?"

"It's the backup generator," Jez explained. "The engine won't run, but this panel here still has power. That's how I was able to control the claws to get you."

"My team will realize we're missing soon enough." Dad said. "There's enough air in here for a few hours at least. We just have to wait it out."

"Uh, there's only one problem with that," Zeke said, looking out of the submersible window.

We all turned to see what Zeke was looking at. Light bubbles **FIZZED** in the water as a dark, looming shadow moved in the distance. Then, out of the shadows burst the monstrous creature, swimming quickly toward us.

"It's the **MEGA SHARK!**" Jez yelled in a shaky voice. "And she's heading straight for us!"

SUNDAY—DUSK

"AAAAAAAAGGGHHH!"

The shark moved toward us with **DEATHLY** speed. She hit us with her nose and sent the submersible **TUMBLING** along the ocean floor.

"We've gotta get out of here!" Zeke cried out.

"But how? We have no power for

the motor," Jez protested. "The only thing that could get us moving would be if something could tow us."

Then an idea hit me. It was a **LONG SHOT,** but it was worth a try.

"Jez, do we have the instrument sounds that my dad was playing on the boat?" I asked.

Jez shrugged, confused. "Yeah, the sound system should work. But now isn't the time for a classical concert, Ari."

"Just play it as **LOUD** as you can," I said. "Trust me."

The shark began to circle us again.

"Do you think it might scare the shark away?" Zeke asked, trying to work out what I was planning.

Jez **BLASTED** the high-pitched piccolo sounds out of the submersible's speaker. The shark didn't seem to care about the noise vibrating through the water.

"It's not working!" Zeke said.

"Just keep going!" I insisted.

The high-pitched sounds continued.
Then, a new **SHADOW** could
be seen from above.

"Another shark?" Zeke stammered.

"I don't think so." I smiled.

Out of the darkness emerged our
friendly pod of **DOLPHINS.**
The shark continued to circle
the submersible and didn't seem
interested in the new arrivals.
The dolphins were quick and
agile, and were perhaps too much

effort for the shark compared to the avatar-lunch hiding in the submersible.

The dolphins swam over and seemed to spot us through the glass. They clicked and **SPUN AROUND,** happy to see us again.

I pressed my nose up against the glass and made direct eye contact with one of them. I was sure it was the same one I played with earlier.

"Can you help us?" I mouthed.

I don't know how I knew it, but the dolphin seemed to understand me. It turned and **SWAM** to the front of the boat.

"Jez, use the claws, but be very, very careful," I instructed.

Jez caught on quick and gently maneuvered the claw to grip the dolphin. The creature didn't thrash or object. It seemed completely calm.

"I think it knows what we are trying to do!" I said.

Another dolphin swam over and nestled itself into the open arms of the second claw. I nodded at Jez and she gently closed it around the dolphin's body.

"Um, guys?" Zeke said. "Whatever you're doing, you'd better hurry. The shark is coming back!"

I blasted the piccolo music even louder.

"LET'S GO!" I yelled.

The dolphins sprang into action, **LAUNCHING** themselves forward to pull the submersible behind them.

I glanced out the back of the submersible and saw that the shark was still following. The pod's remaining three dolphins were **CIRCLING** around her as she continued to pursue us, trying to distract her with their twirling.

"FASTER!" I pleaded to our marine helpers.

They must have understood because they increased their speed. They **WHIZZED** through the ocean, pulling the submersible with ease. The distance between us and the shark began to increase.

"She's **SLOWING DOWN!**" I yelled.

Eventually, the shark dropped back until she disappeared into the murky gray of the ocean.

"**WE DID IT!**" Zeke yelled, pulling Jez and me into a hug.

"Your bravery and knowledge of the sea and its creatures sure helped," Dad croaked from the back seat. "I'm **PROUD** of you, Ari."

I **SMILED** as we continued to whip through the ocean, towed by dolphins, all the way back to shore.

THE FOLLOWING FRIDAY

"So, what **MOVIE** should we watch?" Zeke asked, flicking through the menu on my TV.

"I don't care—as long as it's got **NOTHING** to do with the ocean!" I said.

"Aw, come on, Ari," Dad said from the doorway. "You can't hate the ocean now!"

I **SIGHED.** Dad was right. I didn't hate the ocean—I just didn't want to go back into it for a while.

Turns out, the shark we had found was an **OLD SPECIES** of shark that was long believed to be extinct. Dad's team made the news and got a whole heap of **MONEY** to research it more. They discovered that the mega shark we'd found was pregnant and only looking for a safe place to lay her eggs. No wonder she didn't want us around!

So even though she had tried

to eat me, I finally understood why Dad insisted on respecting the sea. That shark belonged to the ocean. And we were in her **TERRITORY.**

"I think I've got the perfect way to ease you back into the ocean," Dad said. "Why don't you guys come out with me on my **NEXT TRIP?** We've recently discovered an interesting new species out at Cubic Shores."

"New species?" Jez asked, perking up. "What is it?"

"It's a gorgeous blue-striped *Nudibranchia*," Dad said proudly. But when he saw our clueless expressions he added, "It's a new type of **SEA SLUG.**"

Zeke and I **BURST OUT** laughing. Jez scrunched up her face.

It sounded perfect to me—sea slugs weren't likely to eat us!

ALSO AVAILABLE: